Electric eel **Flying fox** **Goose** **Horseshoe crab**

Iguana

June bug

Kangaroo

Leopard seal

Monkey

THE COW IS MOOING ANYHOW

A scrambled alphabet book to be read at breakfast

By Laura Geringer

Pictures by Dirk Zimmer

HarperCollins*Publishers*

The Cow Is Mooing Anyhow
A Scrambled Alphabet Book to Be Read at Breakfast

10 9 8 7 6 5 4 3 2 1
First Edition

Library of Congress Cataloging-in-Publication Data
Geringer, Laura.
The cow is mooing anyhow : a scrambled alphabet book to be read at breakfast / by Laura Geringer; pictures by Dirk Zimmer.
p. cm.
Summary: An influx of rowdy animals representing the letters of the alphabet disrupts a peaceful breakfast.
ISBN 0-06-021986-6. — ISBN 0-06-021987-4 (lib. bdg.)
[1. Animals—Fiction. 2. Alphabet. 3. Stories in rhyme.]
I. Zimmer, Dirk, ill. II. Title.
PZ8.3.G314Co 1991 85-45251
[E]—dc20 CIP
AC

For my father with love

L.G.

To Allie and Natalie

D.Z.

THE COW IS MOOING ANYHOW

BOO

The Iguanas, the iguanas
Come in their pajamas.

The Horseshoe crab, the horseshoe crab
Drives up in a taxicab.

The **G**oose, the goose
Makes me drink my juice.

The **D**ragonfly, the dragonfly
Sprinkles salt as she flies by.

H

I

D

The Terrapin, the terrapin
Takes my eggcup for a spin.

The Puffin, the puffin
Is roosting on my muffin.

G H I

The **M**onkey, the monkey
Dabs my egg with chutney.

D

The **Q**uail, the quail
Complains the cheese is stale.

The **A**lbatross, the albatross
Spreads my toast with applesauce.

T

G H

I

The **X**-ray fish, the x-ray fish
Falls into the butter dish.

M

P

A

D

The **B**ig baboon, the big baboon
Doesn't use a grapefruit spoon.

X

T

G H

I

The **Y**ucca moth, the yucca moth
Chews right through the tablecloth.

The **R**at, the rat
Wears a napkin for a hat.

M

Q P

A B D

Y

X

The Veery, the veery
Is getting very weary.

T R

G H

I

The **Z**um, the zum
Won't spit out his gum.

The **S**lug, the slug
Gets stuck inside my mug.

M

Q P

A B D

Z

Y

X

V

The Leopard seal, the leopard seal
Can't believe this meal's for real.

T S R

G H I M Q P

The Nanny goat, the nanny goat
Calls out for an ice-cream float.

A B D

Z

Y

X

V

The Kangaroo, the kangaroo
Doesn't know just what to do.

T S R

G H

I

The **E**lectric eel, the electric eel
Dives into the oatmeal.

L

M

Q P N

A B D

Z

Y

X

V

The **U**mbrella bird, the umbrella bird
Thinks this breakfast is absurd.

T S R

E G H

The **F**lying fox, the flying fox
Takes cover in the bread box.

The **O**wl, the owl
Is throwing in the towel.

I K L M N

Q P

A B D

Z

Y

X

The June bug, the june bug
Flies around the milk jug.

V

U T S R

E F G H

The **W**ild boar, the wild boar . . .

I

K

L

M

N

O P Q

A B D

Z Y X W V

Opens up the yellow door.

U T S R

E F G H

I

J

K

L

M

Q P O N

A B D

Z

Y

X

W

V

The **C**ow, the cow
Is mooing anyhow.

U T S R

E F G H

I
J
K
L
M

Q P O N

A B C D

Z

Y

X

W

V

U T S R

E F G H

I

J

K

L

M

The End.

Q P O N

Zum

Yucca moth

X-ray fish

Wild boar

Veery

Umbrella bird **Terrapin** **Slug** **Rat**